Hurray for Barbara Park
and the Junie B. Jones books!

"Park, one of the funniest writers around . . . brings her refreshing humor to the beginning chapter-book set." —*Booklist*

"Park convinces beginning readers that Junie B.— *and* reading—are lots of fun."
—*Publishers Weekly*

"Park is simply hilarious."
—America Online's *The Book Report*

"The honesty and inventiveness of this savvy kindergartner make the Junie B. books accessible and completely enjoyable."
—*School Library Journal*

"Park has a wonderful ear for the dialogue of five-year-olds and an even better grasp of how their minds operate." —*Booklist*

"Junie B. Jones is a likable character whose comic mishaps . . . will elicit laughs from young readers."
—*The Horn Book*

"A genuinely funny, easily read story."
—*Kirkus Reviews*

Junie B. Jones Is a Graduation Girl

by Barbara Park

illustrated by Denise Brunkus

SCHOLASTIC INC.

New York   Toronto   London   Auckland   Sydney
Mexico City   New Delhi   Hong Kong   Buenos Aires

ISBN 0-439-32688-5

12 11 10 9 8   11 12 13 14 15 16/0

Printed in the U.S.A.   40

First Scholastic printing, May 2002

Contents

1 / The Month of Junie

My name is Junie B. Jones. The B stands for Beatrice. Except I don't like Beatrice. I just like B and that's all.

I was named after the month of Junie. 'Cause Junie is the month I was born in, of course!

And wait till you hear this!

Yesterday, I finally had my birthday!

AND NOW I AM SIX YEARS OLD!

That day was like magic, I tell you!

'Cause on Saturday night when I went to bed, I was only five years old.

And the next morning—boom!—I WAS SIX!

My grandma Helen Miller had a happy-birthday party for me. She invited my mother and daddy and my grampa Frank Miller.

Also, she invited my baby brother named Ollie. He is seven months old.

He did not add that much.

I loved my party a very lot.

First, I loved my chocolatey cake with white icing. Next, I loved my strawberry ice cream. Plus also, I loved my balloons! And my funny birthday hats. And all my happy-birthday cards!

But mostly . . .

I LOVED MY PRESENTS!

I got five entire boxes to open. And good news! None of them was clothes.

Mostly, I got toys and games. Also, I got a tool belt just my size! Plus my grampa Miller gave me my very own plumbing supplies to help fix the toilet!

But that is not even the end of all my excitement! Because that night—when Mother tucked me into bed—she reminded me that I am graduating from kindergarten on Friday!

My stomach felt jumpy inside when she said that. I quick counted on my fingers.

"But Friday is only five more days," I said.

I did a gulp. "That event sneaked right up on us, didn't it?" I said kind of nervous.

Mother hugged me. "You're not worried, are you, Junie B.?" she asked.

"Graduation will be fun. I promise. And you're going to love first grade."

"But Paulie Allen Puffer says that next year everything will be different," I said. "He says that first grade won't have the same kids as Room Nine does. And so all of our classmates will be weirdo strangers."

Mother did a frown. "No, no, no. That's not true," she said. "I'm sure you'll know a lot of children in your class next year, Junie B. But even if your best friends aren't in your room, you will still be able to play with them at recess. Right?"

I nodded my head kind of slow.

"Yes. I guess so," I said. "Plus Paulie Allen Puffer says that we will be the boss of all the kindergarten kids. So that will be fun, probably. And also, he says our brains and our feet will double in size."

Mother stared at me a real long time. "That Paulie Allen Puffer is a fountain of knowledge," she said very quiet.

After that, we talked some more about graduation and first grade.

And guess what?

The next day at school, my teacher talked about it even *more*.

Her name is Mrs. She has another name, too. But I just like Mrs. and that's all.

Mrs. clapped her hands real happy.

"Well, this is *it,* boys and girls!" she said. "Graduation week is finally here. At seven o'clock on Friday evening, Room Eight and Room Nine will have our graduation ceremony together. And, of course, the children in morning kindergarten will be graduating, too. So every single one of you will receive a diploma!"

I springed out of my chair very thrilled.

"A DIPLOMA! A DIPLOMA! I WILL LOVE A DIPLOMA!" I shouted.

Just then, I did a teensy frown.

"It's not clothes, correct?" I asked.

A meanie boy named Jim laughed real loud.

"Ha! You Gooney Bird Jones! You don't even know what a diploma *is*," he said.

I stamped my foot at that boy.

"Oh yes, I do *too,* Jim," I said. "I know perfectly well what it is. But I am not even the teacher here. And so I will let her explain it to the class."

I sat down and smoothed my skirt. Then I pointed to Mrs.

"Okay, go," I said.

Mrs. wrinkled her eyebrows at me. "As I was about to say, a diploma is a very special piece of paper. A diploma is a certificate that says you've completed part of your education. As you go through school, you'll get several diplomas," she said. "But this one will be your first."

I springed up again. "And guess what else, Mrs.? I am not even afraid of first grade anymore! 'Cause I'll be getting big feet and brains!"

Mrs. said *sit down* to me. Then she told us more about graduation.

She said that as a treat for our families, we will be making them special graduation invitations. And so that will be our activity for the day!

"Yippee!" I said. "I love making invitations, Mrs.! On account of that does not even sound like learning!"

After that, I clapped and clapped.

And all of Room Nine clapped with me.

'Cause graduation week was starting off like a charm!

2/ Rhymes

I sat at my table very nice.

Mrs. passed out colored paper for our invitations.

Also, she passed out curly ribbon. And lace. And paste. And bottles of sparkly glitter.

"Just as a reminder," she said, "we do not paste glitter in our eyebrows. And we do not put lace up our noses. And above all . . . we do *not* glue curly ribbon to our heads and pretend that it's long hair."

She looked and looked at me.

I squirmed in my seat a little bit.

'Cause that woman has a memory like a hawk, I tell you.

Finally, Mrs. went to the board. And she picked up her chalk.

"On the inside of our cards, we're going to write a poem about graduation. Does anyone have any ideas for the first line?"

My friend named Grace waved her hand all around in the air.

"Roses are red! Roses are red!" she called out.

"YES!" hollered Room Nine. "ROSES ARE RED!"

Mrs. smiled. She wrote it on the board for us.

"Okay. Now what about the second line?" she asked.

Room Nine hollered again.

"VIOLETS ARE BLUE! VIOLETS ARE BLUE! VIOLETS ARE BLUE!"

Mrs. wrote that line, too.

"Very good, class," she said. "Now who can think of the third line? Maybe we should try to mention something about *graduation* in this one. Does anyone have any ideas?"

A shy boy named William stood up next to his table.

"Graduation is here," he said kind of nervous.

Mrs. grinned real big. "Excellent job, William! Excellent!"

She printed it on the board.

"All right. There's just one more line to go," she said. "Let's try to make the last word rhyme with the word *blue*, okay?"

She read the first three lines out loud to us.

> "Roses are red,
> Violets are blue.
> Graduation is here . . ."

Room Nine thought and thought.

Then—all of a sudden—rhymes started coming from all over the place!

"My dress will be *new*!" called Lucille.

"My dad's name is *Lou*!" called Jamal Hall.

"We made it! *Woo-hoo!*" called Lynnie.

Just then, Paulie Allen Puffer springed right out of his chair. And he started laughing his head off.

"THE ZOO IS P.U.!" he shouted his loudest.

And then all of Room Nine laughed our

heads off, too! 'Cause *P.U.* is the silliest rhyme we ever heard of!

Mrs. clapped her mad hands together. "Boys and girls! That's *enough*," she grouched.

She hurried to Paulie Allen Puffer's table. And she put him back in his seat.

"I do not appreciate that kind of behavior, young man," she said. "We're trying to write a nice class poem here, Paulie Allen. And your rhyme was entirely inappropriate."

After that, I tried to stop giggling. But that silly poem kept on staying inside my head.

And then, out of nowhere, another funny poem popped right into my brain! And I couldn't even hold it inside me!

I quick jumped up on my chair.

"ROSES ARE RED,
VIOLETS ARE BLUE.
GRADUATION IS HERE,
AND YOUR FEET SMELL LIKE STINK!" I shouted.

After that, Room Nine could not even control themselves again. 'Cause that poem was the funniest thing they ever even heard!

My teacher's eyes got big and wide at me.

"Junie B. Jones! Didn't you hear a word I just said?" she said very annoyed.

Then Mrs. hurried to my table.

And she took me into the hall.

And she pointed me straight to the office.

3 / **A Good Chuckle**

The office is where Principal lives.

I know my way there by heart.

There is a typing lady there, too.

She looked over the counter at me.

"Well, well, well. Would you look who it is," she said.

I looked down at myself. "Well, well, well. It looks like me," I said kind of quiet.

The typing lady pointed at the blue chair.

The blue chair is where bad kids sit.

Only I'm not even bad. But I still have to sit there sometimes.

I put my feet on the edge of the chair. And I hid my face in my knees.

If you don't hide your face, people can recognize yourself.

Finally, I peeked one eye at Principal's door.

And guess what? That guy was looking right back at me!

"Is that Junie B. Jones I see out there?" he asked.

I did a gasp.

'Cause Principal can even recognize me from one eyeball, apparently!

I went into his office. And I sat in the big wood chair.

Principal winked at me.

"I'm a little bit surprised to see you,

Junie B.," he said. "You haven't been sent here for quite some time."

I nodded.

"I know it," I said. "That's because my behavior has shown *considerable improvement*."

I pronounced the words very perfect.

"My teacher printed those words on my report card," I said. "And guess what else showed improvement? My speaking, that's what. 'Cause I don't say *runned* anymore. And I don't say *thinked*. And I don't say *throwed*. Do you want to hear me say them right? Huh? Do you, Principal?"

I took a big breath.

"Ran, ran, ran, ran. Thought, thought, thought, thought. Threw, threw, threw, threw," I said.

I smiled very proud.

"See? I told you. Mother says I am getting a better vocavulary," I said.

"Voca*bu*lary," said Principal.

"Whatever," I said.

Principal smiled. "Yes. Well, I'm delighted with your improvements, Junie B.," he said. "But if everything has gotten better, then why are you here?"

I wiggled in my chair very uncomfortable.

"Because it wasn't my fault, that's why," I said.

"*What* wasn't your fault?" said Principal.

I wiggled some more.

Then, finally, I told Principal about how my teacher made us write a graduation poem. And how she said the last word had to rhyme with blue.

"And so Paulie Allen Puffer rhymed the word *P.U.*," I said. "But then Mrs. got very mad at him. Because she did not appreciate his behavior, young man. Only too bad for me. Because my brain thought of an even sillier poem. And my mouth couldn't hold it inside."

Principal closed his eyes. He did some deep breaths.

"All right," he said. "Let's hear it."

I gulped very worried.

Then I made my voice real soft.

"Roses are red,

Violets are blue.

Graduation is here,

And your feet smell like stink," I said.

After that, Principal kept his eyes closed a real long time. And he did not say any words.

Then, very slow, he put his head down on his desk. And he started to laugh.

His laughing got louder and louder.

And so guess what? Then I started laughing, too!

"That poem was a beaut! Right, Principal? We are having ourselves a good chuckle over this, aren't we?"

Principal stopped laughing very fast. He raised his head again.

"No, Junie B. No. We are *not* having a good chuckle," he said. "I'm sorry. Your poem caught me completely by surprise. But I never should have laughed like that."

He crossed his arms at me.

"You *are* right about one thing, though," he said. "Your poem is definitely silly. But silly things are not always appropriate to say in the classroom, are they?

Your teacher made it clear that she didn't like what Paulie Allen had said, Junie B. But you called out your poem anyway."

He made squinty eyes. "And please don't blame it on your mouth, okay? You know you could have held it inside."

I shrugged my shoulders. "I don't

know," I said kind of quiet. "Maybe I could have."

Principal tapped his fingers on his desk.

"It's a *very* serious matter to disobey a teacher, Junie B.," he said. "And I want you to sit here and think about just how serious it is. Can you do that, please?"

"Yes," I said. "I can."

After that, I squeezed my eyes real tight. And I thought and thought.

Finally, I opened my eyes again. "Good news," I said. "I've said my last *stink*."

Principal nodded his head. "That *is* good news," he said.

Then he stood up. And he held my hand. And he walked me into the hall.

"It's been an interesting year getting to know you, Junie B. Jones," he said. "You're a fascinating little girl."

"Thank you," I said. "You are fasci-nating, too."

After that, both of us waved good-bye. And I started skipping back to Room Nine.

Then, all of a sudden, I stopped. And I spun around.

"Yeah, only we are not saying good-bye forever. Right, Principal? Right? 'Cause next year, I will get sent down here, too, probably. Or else maybe you and I will see each other on the playground. Right?"

Principal did a chuckle.

"Right," he said.

"Hurray!" I said. "Hurray! Hurray!"

Then I turned back around and I skipped to Room Nine my fastest.

'Cause maybe if I hurried, I could still sprinkle glitter on something!

4 / Cats and Gowns

I skipped in the door of Room Nine.

Then my whole face got happy.

'Cause guess who was talking to my teacher?

It was Gus Vallony, that's who!

And Gus Vallony is my favorite janitor!

I zoomed right over to that guy.

"Gus Vallony! Gus Vallony! It is a joy to see you!" I said. "And so what brings you here, anyway?"

Gus Vallony patted my head.

"I had an important delivery to make, sis," he said.

Just then, my bestest friend Lucille came running up to me.

She pointed to a big stack of boxes.

"IT'S CATS AND GOWNS, JUNIE B.!" she shouted. "GUS VALLONY BROUGHT US CATS AND GOWNS!"

She twirled me all around.

"I heard him talking to the teacher! The cats and gowns are right there in those boxes! Everyone is getting one for graduation!" she said.

I jumped up and down at that wonderful news!

'Cause who doesn't love cats? That's what I would like to know!

"CATS AND GOWNS!" I hollered.

"CATS AND GOWNS!" hollered Room Nine.

Mrs. sat down in her chair real slow. Then Gus Vallony patted her shoulder. And he said the word *good luck*.

Mrs. said for Room Nine to please stop shouting.

"I'm sorry, boys and girls. But Lucille did not hear me correctly," she said. "No one in Room Nine is getting a cat and gown for graduation."

Room Nine did a loud groan.

"Then what are we *getting,* exactly?" I asked.

"*Caps* and gowns," said Mrs. "You're all getting a *cap* and gown for graduation. Not *cat* and gown."

"No, no, no!" said Lucille. "I heard you

say *cat*, Teacher! I know I did! I know I did!"

Mrs. said for Lucille to hush. Then she passed out the boxes to all the children.

I looked inside my box real curious.

Then I kept looking and looking. Because something was not right in there.

"My cap got run over by a truck, I think," I said. "It is a big, square flatso."

Mrs. laughed.

Then she came to my table. And she unfolded my cap. And she put it right on my head.

"Hey! What do you know! It fits!" I said.

After that, all of us put on our caps and gowns. And we skipped all around the room.

Only not Lucille. 'Cause she was still

upset about the cat issue, of course.

Pretty soon, the bell was going to ring. And so Mrs. made us put our outfits back in our boxes.

"I'm going to let you take these home with you today," she said. "But please do not play with them on the bus. And don't play with them at home, either. These caps and gowns are *white*, okay? And white material gets soiled very easily."

"I know it, Mrs.!" I said. "I know white material gets soiled easy! 'Cause one time, my grampa Miller spilled beer on his new white tie. And you can still see beer splots on that thing!"

Mrs. looked and looked at me.

Then she sat back down at her desk very quiet.

And she waited for the bell to ring.

5 / A Million Bucks

Me and my bestest friend named Grace rode the bus home together.

We held our boxes very tight on our laps. And we didn't open them.

"We are being careful about our graduation gowns, aren't we, Grace?" I said. "We are being careful not to soil them."

"Yes," said that Grace. "We are."

I looked down at my box. "I am very proud of us for not opening these things," I said.

"I am very proud of us, too," said that Grace.

We rode and rode.

I did a sigh.

"It's too bad we can't just peek at them a little bit, though . . . isn't it, Grace?" I said. "One teensy peek wouldn't even hurt anything, I bet."

That Grace didn't say anything.

I tapped on her.

"Okay, here's what I'm thinking, Grace. I'm thinking we should do one little peek, and that's all," I said. "What do you say, friend?"

Grace made her voice very loud.

"No, Junie B.! No! We are not allowed to! Can't you follow orders? Huh? Do you want to soil these things?"

I did a huffy breath at her.

"But peeking will not even *soil* them, Grace," I said back. "Peeking is just looking with your eyes . . . only faster."

Only too bad for me. Because Grace kept on saying *no, no, no*.

And so I had to wait and wait for that stubborn girl to get off the bus before I could peek.

After she was gone, I looked in my box zippedy quick. And what do you know! I didn't even soil anything!

I got off the bus and ran to my house.

My grandma Helen Miller was babysitting my brother. She was feeding him a snack in his high chair.

"Grandma Miller! Grandma Miller! I got my cap and gown! It is right here in this box!" I said. "Would you like me to try it on for you, Grandma? Huh? Would you?"

Grandma Miller clapped her hands.

"Of course I would!" she said real thrilled. "Try it on right now."

"Okey-doke!" I said.

Then I quick put on my cap and gown. And I danced all around.

"See me, Grandma? See what I look like? I look like a graduation girl!" I said.

I hopped around Ollie's high chair.

"My teacher said not to play in this. But hopping is not the same as playing," I said.

Just then, I heard the front door open.

And hurray, hurray! Mother was home early from work!

Her whole mouth came open when she saw me.

"Oh my goodness!" she said. "Look how *cute* you are!"

"I know it, Mother! I know I am cute!"

I said. "I look like a million bucks in this getup!"

I twirled all around in front of her.

"See me twirling, Mother? Twirling is not the same as playing," I said.

After I stopped twirling, I fell down on the floor.

Falling on the floor is what comes after twirling. It cannot be helped, normally.

Mother picked me up. "Maybe you should take this off before you get it dirty," she said.

"No, Mother. No," I said. "I want to keep it on. Please let me? Please, please!"

I quick ran to Ollie's high chair. And I ducked down behind it.

Ollie peeked around at me.

He had sloppy on his face.

"I am not a sloppy baby like Ollie," I

said. "I won't get this dirty. I promise."

But Mother shook her head.

"I'm sorry, Junie B. But it's just not a good idea to play in your gown," she said.

After that, Mother and Grandma Miller blocked the high chair. And I couldn't run away again.

"Shoot," I said. "I am surrounded."

Mother took my graduation outfit off of me. And she put it back in the box.

Then she put the box way on top of the 'frigerator.

"Let's store it up here for safekeeping," she said.

"Let's not," I said real growly.

Mother made squinty eyes at me. Then she took me by my arm. And she marched me to my room. 'Cause that woman has no sense of humor, apparently.

She shut my door and left.

I flopped on my bed very glum.

My stuffed animals were very glum, too.

"Everybody thinks I am a sloppy baby. But I'm *not*," I said.

"*I don't think you're a sloppy baby*," said my stuffed elephant named Philip Johnny Bob.

"*I don't think you're a sloppy baby, either*," said my Raggedy Ann named Ruth.

My Raggedy Andy named Larry did a sigh. "*I wish your mother didn't put that cap and gown box on top of the 'frigerator,"* he said.

"Me too," said Philip Johnny Bob. *"I wish you could get it down from there so all of us could see it."*

After that, I thought and thought.

Then I lifted up his softie ear.

And I whispered, "Maybe I can."

6/ Pooped and Thirsty

The next morning, my grampa Frank Miller came to baby-sit.

I love that baby-sitter very much!

'Cause he doesn't even follow the rules, that's why!

Grampa Miller let me fix my own breakfast. I fixed two waffles. And three marshmallows. And a bowl of cheese curls.

And guess what else? My grampa let me pour my own grape juice! And I didn't spill one single drop!

"See, Grampa! See how careful I am?"
I said. "I am not a sloppy baby, right?"

Grampa Miller was feeding Ollie.

"Right," he said.

My eyes looked up at the 'frigerator.

I hopped down from my chair.

"All rightie, Frank. I guess I'll be getting
out of your hair now," I said. "If you'll
just hand me that box from the top of the
'frigerator, I will be on my way."

Just then, baby Ollie started to cry.
Grampa Miller patted him.

I tapped my foot. "Yeah, only I'm
waiting, Grampa," I said.

Finally, Grampa Miller stood up and got
my box.

He started to look inside.

Only, all of a sudden, Ollie did a loud
squeal!

And he put his whole bowl of cereal right on his head!

"OH MY GOODNESS!" hollered my grampa.

Then Grampa Miller shoved the box right at me. And he hurried to clean Ollie's head.

I zoomed to my room. Then I locked my door. And I waved my box all around.

"I got it, guys! I got it! I got it!" I said.

"*Hurray!*" said Philip Johnny Bob.

"*Hurray, hurray!*" said Raggedy Ruth and Raggedy Larry.

After that, I set those guys on my bookshelf. And I put on my graduation gown.

"See me, friends?" I said. "See how cute I look? I am a graduation girl! See?"

"*Wowie wow wow!*" they hollered.

After that, I danced and skipped and hopped and twirled. 'Cause they wouldn't stop cheering, that's why!

Finally, I flopped on my bed.

"Okay. That's enough, people," I said. "I am pooped and thirsty."

"*Me too,*" said Raggedy Larry. "*I am pooped and thirsty, too.*"

"*I wish we could get something to drink,*" said Raggedy Ruth.

Just then, a brainstorm came right in my head!

I sat up very straight.

"Hey! Wait a second! I just learned how to pour grape juice without spilling a drop," I said. "And so I can go get us some, maybe!"

"*Yes!*" said Philip Johnny Bob.

"*Yes, yes!*" said Raggedy Ruth and Raggedy Larry.

I hurried to my door and listened in the hall.

Grampa Miller was giving Ollie a bath.

"Shh," I whispered to my friends. "You wait here. I'll be right back."

After that, I tippytoed to the kitchen speedy quick.

And I poured us a cup of grape juice.

And I tippytoed right back again.

7 / Juice Driblets

Grape juice can go wrong.

First, Raggedy Ruth got purple on her mouth.

Then Teddy got a dribble drop on his paw.

And then, oh no, oh no!

RAGGEDY LARRY FORGOT TO SWALLOW HIS WHOLE ENTIRE SIP!

Driblets spilled all over my bookshelf.

I covered my mouth very shocked. Then my heart pounded and pounded. 'Cause if grape juice gets on my rug, I am in BIG TROUBLE, MISSY!

"A cloth! A cloth! I need a cloth!" I hollered.

I ran around and around all over my room. Then, all of a sudden, my eyes looked down at my clothes. And what do you know? I saw all the cloth I needed!

I quick took it off of me. And I soaked up the driblets.

My shoulders felt relief in them.

"Whew! That was a *close* one," I said.

After that, I walked to my bed. And I plopped on my pillow.

"My brain was a genius to think of that," I said.

I breathed and breathed.

Then, all of a sudden, I did a teensy frown.

'Cause something did not feel right here, possibly.

I covered my head with my sheet. Then I turned my head very slow. And I peeked out at my bookshelf.

My stomach did a flip-flop.

Because I saw my graduation gown, that's why! And it had juice driblets soaked into its front!

I looked at Raggedy Larry real mad. "Oh no! Look what you made me do!" I said. "You made me use my graduation gown to soak up that dumb juice. Great, Larry. Just great."

After that, Raggedy Larry got put under my bed. And he did not come out again.

Juice driblets do not go away.

Not even if you erase them with your brand-new eraser. Or if you color them

with your new white crayon. Or if you
brush them with Daddy's new whitening,
brightening toothpaste.

I brushed up and down and all around.
But the driblets did not budge.

"Shoot!" I said. "Now I will look like a

sloppy baby at graduation! And I'm not even the one who *dribbled*!"

Just then, I heard a knock on my door.

It was Grampa Miller!

"Junie B.? Is everything okay in there?" he said.

My heart got very pounding again.

"Yes, Grampa! Yes! Everything is perfectly perfect!" I hollered. "I am just playing with my stuffed animals, and that's all."

Grampa Frank Miller knocked some more.

"Could you open the door, please?" he asked.

I felt tension in me. 'Cause I didn't want him to see my problem, that's why.

I quick pushed my graduation gown under my bed. Then I opened my door a teensy crack.

"Hello. How are you today?" I said. "I am fine. Except I am right in the middle of something. So I would like to get back to it, please."

Grampa Miller was holding baby Ollie. He looked disappointed at me.

"Oh phooey," he said. "Now that I've got your brother cleaned up, I thought maybe you and I could teach him how to play checkers."

I looked at Ollie. He was wearing a clean shirt with purple polka dotties.

"No thank you," I said. "Maybe I'll teach him checkers some other day."

I waved at my grampa Miller very sweet.

"Well, nice seeing you again, Frank. Good-bye," I said.

After that, I closed the door. And I waited for Grampa's footsteps to leave.

Finally, I pulled my graduation gown from under the bed. And I stared and stared at that stupid thing.

"Why did this dumb gown have to be white?" I grouched. "Why couldn't it be purple like the grape juice? If it was purple like the grape juice, the driblets would blend right in."

I tapped my fingers real annoyed.

"Or why couldn't this dumb gown have purple flowers on it? The juice would blend in with flowers, too, I bet," I said. "Or what about polka dotties like Ollie's shirt? If there were purple polka dotties, no one would notice the driblets, for sure."

Just then, I sat up very fast.

'Cause I was getting another brainstorm in my head, I believe.

I zoomed straight to my desk.

Then I looked through all my drawers. And I found my colored markers.

I laughed real happy.

Then I spread my graduation gown on the floor. And I worked and worked very hard.

And guess what?

When I finally got done, you couldn't even spot the driblets, hardly!

"My brain is a genius after all!" I said.

After that, I put my cap and gown in the box again. And I took it back to my grampa Miller.

"All rightie, Grampa," I said. "You can put this back on the 'frigerator now, please."

Then I smiled real big.

Because guess what else?

He did!

8 / Getting Ready

Room Eight and Room Nine practiced for graduation together.

We practiced on the stage in the auditorium. 'Cause a stage is where people get diplomas, of course!

Mrs. showed everyone how to walk up the steps without tripping. She played music for us to march in with.

And guess what?

Room Nine marched better than Room Eight. Except Paulie Allen Puffer kept bowing real silly. And Lynnie kept stepping on people's heels. Plus shy William ran out of the auditorium. And down the hall. And Gus Vallony had to chase him around the parking lot.

After that, Principal talked to William a real long time. Plus also, his mother was called in, I believe.

"I am not like William," I told Lucille and Grace. "I am not even nervous of walking up on that stage, hardly."

"Me neither," said that Grace. "I am not nervous of walking up on that stage, hardly, either."

Lucille fluffed her fluffy hair. "My nanna says that I was *born* to be on the stage," she said. "Nanna says that people enjoy looking at me. Because I am a feast for their eyes."

After that, Lucille wrinkled her nose very cute. And she skipped around and around in a circle.

Grace and I watched her for a real long time.

Then, finally, Lucille stopped skipping. And all of us hugged and hugged.

'Cause we are the bestest three friends I ever even saw.

Graduation week went by very fast.

Friday night came in a jiffy. I felt so excited, I couldn't even eat my dinner that good.

I got down from my chair. And I ran and ran all over the house.

"Settle down," said Daddy.

"Settle down," said Mother.

"Settle down!" I hollered.

Then I laughed real loud. 'Cause I am a hoot, that's why!

Finally, it was time to go.

Mother got my graduation box off the top of the 'frigerator.

I jumped up and down.

"Let *me* carry that, Mother! Please, please, please? I want to carry my box to Room Nine myself. 'Cause that's where all of us are getting dressed."

Mother handed me the box.

Then Daddy said, "Settle down" again. And all of us drove to my school.

Grampa and Grandma Miller met us in the parking lot.

I hugged them hello. Then I zoomed to Room Nine speedy fast.

And guess what?

All of the children from morning and

afternoon kindergarten were getting ready together!

I ran through the door. "IT'S ME, PEOPLE! IT'S JUNIE B. JONES! I AM HERE FOR GRADUATION!"

Lucille and Grace came rushing over.

They were already wearing their caps and gowns. And they looked marvelous, I tell you!

"Hurry up, Junie B.," said Lucille. "Hurry up and put on your cap and gown. Our teacher is going to take our picture."

"Yes!" said that Grace. "Hurry! Hurry!"

She quick grabbed my box away from me. And she took out my cap and gown.

Grace did a gasp.

"Oh no, Junie B.! What happened?" she said. "What happened to your cap and gown?"

My stomach felt squeezy and sickish. 'Cause that outfit looked spottier than I remembered.

"Put it *down*, Grace," I said. "Don't show people. I don't want anyone to notice."

Lucille laughed very loud.

"But that's so dumb, Junie B.," she said. "How could people not notice? You colored big purple splotchies all over your graduation clothes."

I did a huffy breath at that girl.

"Those are not big *splotchies,* Lucille," I said. "Those are purple polka dotties that I drew to blend in my juice driblets. And that is a whole different ball game, madam!"

Just then, some of the children heard me yelling. They turned to look.

"*Great,* Lucille," I said. "*Now* look what you did. You called attention to myself! And so now how can I even blend in?"

After that, I quick grabbed my graduation gown. And I ran to the back of the room.

Just then, I heard a voice.

"Junie B. Jones?"

I looked to the front of the room.

It was my teacher.

Mrs. stretched her neck to look back at me. "Is there a *problem* back there, Junie B.?" she asked.

I shook my head real fast.

"No, Mrs.! No!" I said. "There isn't a problem. I promise! And so please do not come back here. And I *mean* it."

Mrs. came back there.

And what do you know . . .

All of Room Nine came with her.

Mrs. took my cap and gown out of my hands.

The children laughed and laughed at that thing.

"What kind of dumb gown do you call that?" said Meanie Jim.

"*I* know!" said Paulie Allen Puffer. "It's the kind of gown that a clown would wear!"

"Yeah!" shouted Jim. "It's a purple, spotty *clown* gown!"

After that, the laughing got louder and louder.

I put my hands over my ears to keep it out of my head.

Then I tried to tell them about Raggedy Larry. And the driblets. And my purple colored marker. But my nose started running very much. And I couldn't even talk that good.

Finally, I started to cry.

And guess what?

Then nobody laughed anymore.

9/The Time of My Life

Mrs. took me into the hall.

She wiped my face with a tissue. And we talked about my graduation gown.

Mrs. said I would look darling in that dotty thing. 'Cause purple is her favorite color. Plus grape juice is her favorite kind of drink.

I kept on crying.

'Cause I didn't actually buy it, that's why.

Pretty soon, Mother and Daddy came

hurrying to Room Nine. They brought Grampa Miller with them.

Their eyes popped out at my spotty, dotty gown.

"I'm sorry, I'm sorry. Please don't yell at me," I said. "'Cause I'm already crying, see? Plus wearing this dumb clown gown will be punishment enough."

Mother and Daddy didn't yell. They said we would talk about this problem later.

After that, Mother helped me put on my cap and gown. And she hugged me very nice.

Then Daddy grinned. And he said I look cute in dots.

"She does look cute," said Grampa Miller. "And not only that, but when she goes on the stage, she'll be easy to *spot*."

He winked at me.

I did a giggle. 'Cause that man is a silly joker, that's why.

Finally, Mrs. patted me.

"Are you feeling better now, Junie B.?" she asked. "Are you ready to go back inside and be with your friends?"

I shrugged kind of worried.

"Sure she is! Of course she is!" said my grampa. "My goodness! This is Junie B. Jones!"

After that, he stood me up straight and tall. And he faced me to my classroom.

Then I breathed in a big breath.

And me and Mrs. went back into Room Nine.

Paulie Allen and Jim jumped out at me.

"SURPRISE!" they hollered. "SURPRISE! SURPRISE!"

"SURPRISE!" hollered my bestest friend named Grace.

I looked at those people very shocked. Then my mouth came all the way open!

'Cause THEY HAD DOTS ON THEIR CLOTHES! JUST LIKE MINE!

That Grace skipped all around.

"It was Jim's idea, Junie B.!" she said. "Jim said that if all of us have spots, too, then you will feel better! And so Paulie Allen Puffer found the colored markers! And we colored our caps and gowns just like yours!"

Grace looked at Mrs.

"See us, Teacher? Aren't we beautiful? I colored red spots. And Jim colored blue spots. And Paulie Allen Puffer colored green spots," she said.

Just then, William raised his hand. "And

I'm coloring orange spots," he said kind of soft.

"And I'm coloring lavender spots!" said Charlotte.

"And I'm coloring pink spots!" said my bestest friend Lucille. "'Cause pink brings out the natural blush of my cheeks."

Mrs. smiled.

Her smile kept on getting bigger.

"Well, Junie B. Jones?" she said finally. "What do you think about all of this? Hmm?"

My face beamed very joyful.

"I THINK I LOVE THESE PEOPLE! THAT'S WHAT I THINK!" I hollered.

Then Jim said, "Gross!"

And Paulie Allen Puffer said, "Gross!" too.

After that, all of Room Nine laughed and laughed.

And this time . . . even me!

Graduation finally got started.

The Room Eight teacher walked up the steps of the stage. She said hello to all the people.

Then Mrs. walked up the steps of the stage, too. She was still smiling.

"Families and friends . . . I've been a teacher for a very long time," she said. "But in all my years of teaching, these are some of the most *colorful* graduates I've ever seen."

Mrs. held out her arms.

"Ladies and gentlemen, we are proud to

present the graduates of Room Eight and Room Nine."

Just then, the music started. And all of the children walked into the auditorium.

The audience chuckled at us very happy.

Room Nine chuckled back at them.

After that, all of us sat in special chairs. And both of the teachers talked and talked some more.

And then, it finally happened!

Mrs. started to call our names! And one by one we walked up on the stage. And we got our diplomas!

And good news!

Paulie Allen Puffer did not bow real silly. And Lynnie did not step on people's heels. And shy William did not run away.

It was the time of our life, I tell you!

I felt a billion feet tall up there.

When Mrs. gave me my diploma, she shook my hand real nice.

"I'm going to miss you, Junie B. Jones," she said. "You are truly one of a kind."

"Thank you, Mrs.," I said. "You are truly one of a kind, too."

After that, my grampa Frank Miller did a loud whistle. And Mother and Daddy clapped very proud.

And here is the happiest news of all!

When graduation was over, Room Nine did not even have to say good-bye to each other! Because all of us are coming back to this same school for first grade! So we can play at recess, just like Mother said!

And guess what else?

I can't *wait* to see those guys again!

Because we will be friends forever and forever.

And always and always.

And I *mean* it.

Junie B. has a lot to say

about everything and everybody . . .

the school bus

The bus made a big roar. Then a big puff of black smelly smoke came out the back end of it. It's called bus breath, I think.

• from *Junie B. Jones and the Stupid Smelly Bus*

waffles

Grampa Miller cooked them for me! And he let me pour on my own syrup. And he didn't yell whoa! whoa! whoa!

• from *Junie B. Jones and a Little Monkey Business*

Room Nine

My table is where I sit up straight. And do my work. And don't talk to my neighbor. Except I keep on forgetting that part.

• from *Junie B. Jones and Some Sneaky Peeky Spying*

That Grace

Me and that Grace ride the school bus together. She has my favorite kind of hair. It is called *automatically curly.*

• from *Junie B. Jones Loves Handsome Warren*

. . . in Barbara Park's other
Junie B. Jones books!

class pictures
The class picture is when all of Room Nine lines up in two rows. The biggie kids stand in the back. And the shortie kids stand in the front. I am a shortie kid. Only that is nothing to be ashamed of.
• from *Junie B. Jones Has a Monster Under Her Bed*

speed
Jiffy is the nickname for speedy quick.
• from *Junie B. Jones Smells Something Fishy*

grown-up words
Whatever is the grown-up word for *that is the dumbest thing I ever heard.*
• from *Junie B. Jones Has a Peep in Her Pocket*

phone numbers
Its name is 555-5555. And that was a hard number to remember, I tell you! 'Cause I kept forgetting the five.
• from *Junie B. Jones Is Captain Field Day*

Barbara Park says:

66 When I wrote the first adventure of Junie B. Jones, my plan was to keep her in kindergarten forever. 'Almost six' seemed exactly the right age for a spunky little girl who could *almost* keep her slightly outrageous personality under control . . . but not *quite*.

Then, little by little, I began to change my mind. After all, part of the fun of going to school is knowing that your hard work will be rewarded at the end of the year by a promotion to the next grade level. And Junie B. has definitely come a long way since the first day she rode the 'stupid smelly bus' to kindergarten.

So hurray! Graduation Day has finally arrived for Room Nine! And, of course, when Junie B. Jones is part of the ceremony, things *almost* go smoothly . . . but not *quite*. **99**